W9-CHK-093

SPIDER-MAN VERSUS SANDMAN

Adapted by Harry Lime
Illustrated by Steven E. Gordon
Screenplay by Alvin Sargent
Screen Story by Sam Raimi & Ivan Raimi
Based on the Marvel Comic Book by Stan Lee and Steve Ditko

HarperCollins*Publishers*

COLUMBIA PICTURES PRESENTS A MARVEL STUDIOS/LAURA ZISKIN PRODUCTION A SAM RAIMI FILM TOBEY MAGUIRE "SPIDER-MAN 3" KIRSTEN DUNST JAMES FRANCO THOMAS HADEN CHURCH TOPHER GRACE BRYCE DALLAS HOWARD THEMES BY DANNY ELFMAN SCORE BY CHRISTOPHER YOUNG EXECUTIVE PRODUCERS STAN LEE KEVIN FEIGE JOSEPH M. CARACCIOLO BASED ON THE MARVEL COMIC BOOK BY STAN LEE AND STEVE DITKO

MARVEL SPIDER-MAN CHARACTER TM & © 2006 MARVEL CHARACTERS, INC. ALL RIGHTS RESERVED.

SCREEN STORY BY SAM RAIMI & IVAN RAIMI SCREENPLAY BY ALVIN SARGENT PRODUCED BY LAURA ZISKIN AVI ARAD GRANT CURTIS DIRECTED BY SAM RAIMI COLUMBIA PICTURES

sony.com/Spider-Man

HarperCollins®, ®, and I Can Read Book® are trademarks of HarperCollins Publishers.

Spider-Man 3: Spider-Man Versus Sandman Spider-Man and all related characters: ™ & © 2007 Marvel Characters, Inc. Spider-Man 3, the movie: © 2007 Columbia Pictures Industries, Inc. All rights reserved. Printed in the United States of America. No part of this book may be used or reproduced in any manner whatsoever without written permission except in the case of brief quotations embodied in critical articles and reviews.

For information address HarperCollins Children's Books, a division of HarperCollins Publishers,
1350 Avenue of the Americas, New York, NY 10019.
www.icanread.com

Library of Congress catalog card number: 2006934364
ISBN-10: 0-06-083722-5 — ISBN-13: 978-0-06-083722-8
Book design by Rick Farley

❖ First Edition

SPIDER-MAN 3™

Today is Spider-Man's big day.
Everyone is here to thank a hero,
Spider-Man.

That's me.

Most of the time I am Peter Parker,

just a regular guy.

But today I am Spider-Man.

It looks like the whole city is here.

Old people, young people.

Nice people.

And some not very nice people, too.

I can see Sandman with
my Spidey sense.
He is about to make some trouble.

I always liked playing in the sand
when I was a kid.
But I don't like Sandman.

Sandman is huge.

If I don't stop him,

some of these people will get hurt.

That truck is full of money.

The driver is bringing it to the bank.

It looks like Sandman wants
to withdraw some money right now.
But the money doesn't belong to him.

I have to stop him!

It's time for me to go to work.

I cannot enjoy my party

if a bad guy is planning a crime.

Sandman is stealing
other people's money.

Most of the time,

when I fight bad guys, they give up.

But Sandman is a tricky guy!
First Sandman turns into sand.

Then Sandman jumps into the truck
and takes off.

I think I'll go along for the ride.

Sandman may be made of sand,
but he punches very hard!
That hurt!

I land on the back door of the truck.
Zooming down the street this way
feels like water-skiing.

I can’t let Sandman get away
with that money.
But my job is to protect the people
of this city.

I will do anything to help the people.
That's the most important thing of all.

And little kids need protection
more than anyone.

It's time to go to work!

I need to stop Sandman

and get this truck under control.

I'll say good-bye to Sandman for now.
This little girl needs my help.
But I won't let Sandman get away for long.

Helping people is the best part of my job.

I like to make people happy.

And now it's time to find Sandman!

Dear Parent:
Your child's love of reading starts here!

Every child learns to read in a different way and at his or her own speed. Some go back and forth between reading levels and read favorite books again and again. Others read through each level in order. You can help your young reader improve and become more confident by encouraging his or her own interests and abilities. From books your child reads with you to the first books he or she reads alone, there are I Can Read Books for every stage of reading:

SHARED READING
Basic language, word repetition, and whimsical illustrations, ideal for sharing with your emergent reader

BEGINNING READING
Short sentences, familiar words, and simple concepts for children eager to read on their own

READING WITH HELP
Engaging stories, longer sentences, and language play for developing readers

READING ALONE
Complex plots, challenging vocabulary, and high-interest topics for the independent reader

ADVANCED READING
Short paragraphs, chapters, and exciting themes for the perfect bridge to chapter books

I Can Read Books have introduced children to the joy of reading since 1957. Featuring award-winning authors and illustrators and a fabulous cast of beloved characters, I Can Read Books set the standard for beginning readers.

A lifetime of discovery begins with the magical words **"I Can Read!"**

Visit www.icanread.com for information on enriching your child's reading experience.